D0527185

Servic

80 001 721 031

Northamptonshire Libraries & Information Service	
Peters	08-Aug-01
CF	£4.50

Published in Great Britain in 2001 by Hodder Wayland,
an imprint of Hodder Children's Books

Text copyright © 2001 Sam Godwin
Illustrations copyright © 2001 Alison Astill

The right of Sam Godwin to be identified as the author of
this Work and the right of Alison Astill to be identified as the
illustrator of this Work has been asserted by them in accordance
with the Copyright, Designs and Patents Act 1988.

All rights reserved. No part of this publication may be reproduced,
stored in a retrieval system, or transmitted, in any form or by any
means without the prior written permission of the publisher, nor
be otherwise circulated in any form of binding or cover other than
that in which it is published and without a similar condition being
imposed on the subsequent purchaser.

British Library Cataloguing in Publication Data
Godwin, Sam
The prince in the Crystal Palace : a story about Prince Albert.
- (Historical storybooks)
1.Albert, Prince Consort of Victoria, Queen of Great Britain
- Juvenile fiction 2.Great Britain - History - Victoria, 1837-1901
- Juvenile fiction 3.Historical fiction 4.Children's stories
I.Title II.Astill, Alison
823.9'14[J]

ISBN 0 7502 3297 8

Printed in Hong Kong by Wing King Tong Co. Ltd.

Hodder Children's Books,
A division of Hodder Headline Limited,
338 Euston Road,
London NW1 3BH

The Prince in the Crystal Palace

Sam Godwin

Illustrated by Alison Astill

an imprint of Hodder Children's Books

Prince Albert (1819-1861)

26 October 1819 Prince Albert was born near Coburg in Germany. His father was the Duke of Saxe-Coburg-Gotha, and his mother was a princess.

10 February 1840 Albert married his cousin Queen Victoria of England. Their marriage was a very happy one and they had nine children. Over the years, Queen Victoria came to rely a great deal on her husband's advice. Prince Albert helped improve the lives of working children in Victorian England. He also took an active interest in art, science and industry.

1850 Albert became chairman of the commission appointed to organize the Great Exhibition of All Nations at the Crystal Palace in Hyde Park.

1 May 1851 The Great Exhibition opened and continued until 15 October that year. It was a massive success and made enough profit to buy land for the building of several museums in London as well as the Royal Albert Hall.

1857 Prince Albert was created Prince Consort.

14 December 1861 Albert died of typhoid at the age of 42 at Windsor Castle. Queen Victoria was inconsolable.

Chapter 1
'Not for the Likes of Us'

'A Crystal Palace,' said my mother wearily, giving Uncle Herbert a slice of meat pie and a glass of beer for his supper. 'Whatever will they think of next?'

'It's going to be grand,' said Uncle Herbert. 'A wonderful exhibition, housed in a building such as has never been seen before. They reckon there are going to be some 13,000 exhibits from every corner of the globe.' He turned to me. 'You'll like it, George. All those new inventions they're going to put on show.'

My eyes lit up. I've always been fascinated by machines, especially ones that move. My dream is to invent a carriage that flies through the air, propelled by an engine of my own design. But my mother is a devout Christian and does not approve of science. And my father drives a hansom cab for a living. I'm expected to take over the business when he retires. But I've never had a way with horses, nor any sense of direction – which is important for a cab driver. I'd much rather be an inventor, someone who leaves his mark on the world.

Uncle Herbert finished his pie and sipped his beer. He was a policeman, one of those chosen to keep thieves away from the Crystal Palace building site in Hyde Park. Ever since his wife had died, he'd been living with us.

'Prince Albert's already been to the site twice, you know,' said Uncle Herbert. 'This exhibition is very close to his heart. He says that it will show the whole world where art and industry stand in the middle of the nineteenth century. We're on the edge of a wonderful new world, Prince Albert says. Science is making life better, not just for the rich but for the poor too. Who knows where it will all lead?'

'Not to heaven, that's for sure,' my mother said. 'All this sinful talk about art and invention. We should put our trust in the Lord, not in science.'

Uncle Herbert sighed. 'Next time I'm on day shift, I'll take you to Hyde Park with me, George,' he said. 'You can have a look round. And, who knows, you might even meet Prince Albert yourself. You could show him your design for that flying machine.'

'Stop filling the boy's head with nonsense, Herbert,' said my mother. 'His father will be very angry with him if he finds out he's been wasting time drawing and sketching.'

She took Uncle Herbert's empty plate and started washing it at the sink. We only have one plate in the house and my father was due home for his supper any minute.

'But Prince Albert says...' began Uncle Herbert.

'I've heard enough about royalty for one night,' Mother cut in. 'You put your helmet on and go to work, Herbert. And you, George, go down to the cellar and fetch me a shovelful of coal, if there's any left. And then get yourself to bed. Forget about Prince Albert and his wonderful new world. It's not for the likes of us.'

Chapter 2
Prince or Vampire?

I lay on my bed and thought about Prince Albert. What did I know about him? He had married Queen Victoria in 1840, the same year I was born. The royal couple had seven children, three boys and four girls.

His Royal Highness took a great interest in science. Uncle Herbert said he was even trying to better the lot of working children. To my knowledge, no member of the royal household had ever shown the slightest interest in the welfare of poor children before. I felt Prince Albert was different.

Downstairs, the front door opened and my father came in. I heard him take off his boots, grunting as he tugged on them. Mother set his dinner on the table.

'Been a good night, Edward?' she asked.

Father jingled the coins in his pocket. 'Not bad.'

There was a knock on the back door and I heard Mrs Ethel Brown, our rather plump neighbour, come into the kitchen.

'Have you some sugar I could borrow, Maud?' she asked my mother. Ethel often popped round to borrow something and usually liked to have a gossip. 'I've been hearing all about the Great Exhibition and the Crystal Palace,' she said. 'All that glass. All those iron girders. It can't possibly be safe. You won't catch me going anywhere near it.'

'It'll be good for business,' said my father, his mouth full of pie. 'The authorities are expecting millions to visit the exhibition.'

'Millions?' cried Ethel. 'Where are they going to put them all?'

'It'll bring in foreign money,' continued Father. 'There's going to be visitors from all over the world.'

'Foreigners!' exclaimed Ethel. 'London will be crawling with them. I'm going to put an extra lock on my front door. Don't want any of 'em going near my Constance.'

'My brother Herbert says he met Prince Albert in Hyde Park,' Mother said.

'I shouldn't like to meet Prince Albert in the park,' scoffed Ethel. 'They say he's got small red eyes, just like a vampire.'

'Red eyes?' said my father, puzzled.

'They might not show it on the mugs,' said Ethel, 'but Mr Humphreys the butcher has read about it in *The Sketch*, so it must be true.'

Poor Prince Albert, I thought. It can't be very nice having small red eyes like a vampire…

Chapter 3
'Curiosity and Imagination'

My first chance to see the Crystal Palace came a week later. Mother had gone down to Brighton to visit my Aunt Peggy, who'd been taken ill after eating stale oysters. Father was out working all the time. The Great Exhibition was almost ready, foreign visitors had already started pouring into London, and the cabbies were busy ferrying them around the city day and night.

'Would you like to come to Hyde Park with me, George?' Uncle Herbert asked one morning.

I raced upstairs to put on my best jacket and tucked my folder under my arm. It wasn't a real folder, just two sheets of thick cardboard held together with glue. I had begged them off the grocer.

'You'll have to keep out of everybody's way, mind,' said Uncle Herbert as we walked along the crowded streets to the park. 'I don't want to get in trouble with the super.'

As we reached Hyde Park, people swarmed around us, carrying tools, many calling to each other in foreign languages. I saw men in flowing robes and others in mandarin hats. Burly soldiers in uniform hurried along carrying enormous wooden chests. Then, suddenly, I saw the Crystal Palace.

It was dazzling. All its glass panes, held together by steel rods, shone in the spring sunlight. I gazed up at it in admiration, envying Joseph Paxton, the brilliant man who had designed it. I remembered reading in a magazine that the building was 1,848 feet long and 408 feet wide. It looked enormous. Would I ever create anything so magnificent, I wondered?

'Don't get lost, will you?' said Uncle Herbert. 'I've got to report for duty but I'll meet you by the entrance again in two hours.'

'I'll be here,' I said. He marched off and I wandered around, watching people putting the exhibits in place. I'd never seen so many things gathered together in my life. There were toys and clothes, chairs, tables and ornaments, china dishes and silver cutlery, richly coloured carpets and curtains, stuffed animals and canoes. Giant trees scraped against the glass roof.

There were machines too – more machines than I could possibly sketch in a year. Farm machines, steam machines, hydraulic machines that deafened you with their noise. There was even a machine that made envelopes. I stared at it in disbelief.

'Wonderful isn't it?' said a voice behind me. I turned and saw an elegantly dressed gentleman with huge sideburns. He spoke with a funny accent, so I guessed right away that he must be an exhibitor, sent by some foreign monarch to look after his country's artefacts.

'I wish *I'd* invented it,' I said.

The gentleman smiled. 'Perhaps you could invent another machine. One that made greeting cards to go in the envelopes.' He laughed at his own joke.

'I'd like to invent a flying machine,' I blurted out.

'Now that's an interesting idea,' said the gentleman. 'Would it go far?'

'Right across the sea,' I answered, carried away by his interest.

I took out my sketches to show him. 'Look, I've made a few drawings.'

He studied my work closely. 'This is very good,' he said. 'Not at all practical, but you're still young. You might become an inventor yet. You certainly possess the two most important qualities a scientist must have: curiosity and imagination.'

Then a man in a black frock coat came up to him and whispered in his ear. The gentleman looked at his pocket watch. 'You'll have to excuse me, young man,' he said. 'I have a meeting in five minutes.'

I wanted to thank him. But, before I could speak, he was gone.

Chapter 4
George Gets Into Trouble

I was full of excitement. I'd finally met someone who approved of my dreams and ambitions. Now I was determined to be an inventor – I would work day and night at my inventions.

But my father only laughed when I told him about the foreign gentleman and what he had said to me. As more people poured into London, he started to take me out on his evening cab rounds. My teacher at school complained that I was tired all the time but that didn't seem to bother my father.

'Pay attention, you'll need to know the streets of London by heart,' he would say as we travelled along the gas-lit streets. I would nod obediently but he knew my heart wasn't in it.

Everything came to a head one Saturday night, just a week before the opening of the Great Exhibition. Father had been working round the clock, only coming home once a day for a quick mutton sandwich and a glass of ale. Mother, who'd returned from Brighton, was worried about him.

'You have a nap before you go out again, Edward,' she said. 'It'll do you the world of good.'

'I daren't,' said my father. 'I've got to pick up a German gentleman from the docks in two hours. Can't run the risk of missing the job.'

'George'll wake you up on time,' my mother assured him.

'Very well, then,' my father said, 'but I need to get going by nine at the latest.' He sat back in an armchair and stretched out his legs. His eyes drooped shut.

Mother put on her shawl. She was going to church with Ethel. 'Now don't forget to wake up your father at half eight,' she warned.

I promised her I wouldn't forget and brought out my sketchbook from its hiding place under the bed. That day I'd had the idea of constructing a machine that would peel potatoes with the aid of a water pump. It wasn't a grand invention but I thought it could work.

As I got absorbed in my sketching, I lost all track of time. The clock on the mantelpiece ticked on, but I took no notice. Suddenly my father jumped out of the armchair.

'What time is it?'

I looked up at the clock, panic building in my throat. 'Just gone nine,' I said hoarsely.

Anger spread across my father's face. I could tell he was going to hit me if I didn't run out of the room. 'You were supposed to wake me up at half eight,' he snarled. My father didn't often lose his temper. But, when he did, he was deadlier than a jungle snake.

'Get my boots,' he ordered. I ran to the kitchen to fetch them.

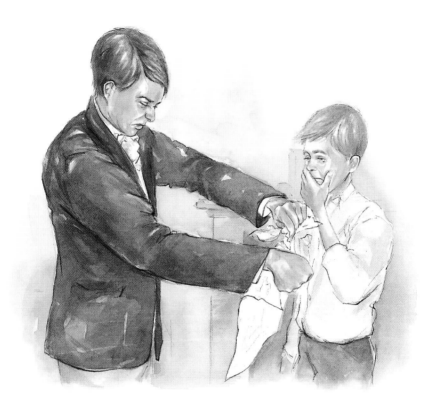

When I returned, he was holding my
sketchbook. 'Is this why you forgot to
wake me up?' he demanded. Before I could
answer, he tore up the drawings. 'Don't let
me catch you wasting your time on these
foolish notions again,' he said.

'But the foreign gentleman…' I began.

'When are you going to understand?' my father roared. 'Poor people like us don't invent things. We work hard to make ends meet. That's how it's always been, and that's how it will be till the end of time.' And with that he threw my torn sketch-book into the fire.

I was filled with despair as I watched it burn. Would I have to forget my dream of becoming an inventor?

Chapter 5
The Great Day Arrives

Uncle Herbert had been given free tickets for the opening of the Grand Exhibition. At last the day had come – 1 May 1851. After breakfast we all started walking towards Hyde Park. It seemed as if the entire world was heading in the same direction.

'Thousands and thousands of tickets have been sold,' said Uncle Herbert proudly. 'The exhibition is already a great success.'

'I wonder if Princess Victoria will be there,' said Constance, Ethel's daughter.

'I'm sure she will,' said her mother.

Princess Victoria was Prince Albert's eldest daughter, and some said his favourite.

'How will we recognize her?' Constance asked Uncle Herbert.

'She'll be standing next to Prince Albert,' said my mother.

Constance fanned her face with a handkerchief. 'And how will we recognize him?'

Her mother laughed. 'He'll be the one with the small red eyes.'

When we reached Hyde Park, Uncle Herbert spoke to one of the officials who let us go through to the front. A platform had been set up inside the palace, with chairs for the royal family. There was a hush as Queen Victoria swept past us towards the palace, followed by a young girl who Constance took to be Princess Victoria, and a boy who my mother was sure was the young Prince of Wales. With them was a man with huge sideburns.

'That's the gentleman who encouraged me to keep working on my inventions,' I gasped.

'Don't be silly,' said my mother.

'But it *is* him,' I argued. 'I didn't recognize him because I was expecting to see a man with small red eyes! And he spoke with an accent. I'd forgotten Prince Albert was German.'

My father glowered at me. 'Be quiet,' he said. 'We'll have none of your silly fantasies today. Listen, the opening ceremony has just started.'

We couldn't hear the prince's speech but we could see him through the glass. Later I read in a newspaper that he spoke about bringing the nations of the world closer together. He told us about his hopes for the future, a future based on science and industry.

I should have enjoyed the ceremony but inside I was furious. I *had* spoken to Prince Albert. But no one believed me.

After the prince's speech, Queen Victoria cut the ribbon. Suddenly all the fountains in the park came to life, some of them shooting jets of water 250 feet up into the air. The crowds clapped and cheered.

At last the Great Exhibition of All Nations was open.

Chapter 6
Inside the Crystal Palace

I'd already seen inside the Crystal Palace but nothing could have prepared me for the sight that now met my eyes. The exhibition was divided into courts, every one of them showing exhibits from different countries. There was one devoted to Ancient Egypt, another to Indian art and yet another to German inventions. All around us were huge statues towering above the crowds. And right in the middle of the palace was another fountain, a perfumed one, bigger than any of the ones outside.

In one of the courts, we came upon a diamond the size of my fist. 'It's called the Koh-i-noor,' explained Uncle Herbert. 'The name means "Mountain of Light".'

'It was found in the pocket of an eight-year-old Sikh ruler after a battle with the British in India,' I added, reading the label. 'It's very famous.'

'I heard it was cursed,' muttered Ethel.

In another part of the exhibition, we saw a huge model of Liverpool Docks. As we gazed at it in wonder, a hush fell on the crowd. Queen Victoria and Prince Albert were approaching the exhibit, accompanied by courtiers and other gentlemen. Constance gasped as she caught sight of Princess Victoria again. The princess looked beautiful in her lacy white frock, with a crown of flowers on her head.

The royal family moved closer towards us, the Queen accepting bunches of flowers from admirers. Suddenly Prince Albert was standing in front of me, smiling.

'Hello, young man,' he said, shaking my hand. 'How are your sketches coming along?

What are you working on now?'

'A potato peeling machine,' I stammered.

I could almost hear Ethel's jaw drop.
'His eyes are brown, not red,' she whispered
to my mother.

'That sounds very useful,' Prince Albert
said to me. 'Keep at it.'

He turned to Uncle Herbert, thinking he was my father. 'You have a fine son, sir. Do encourage him in his efforts. The world is an exciting place for a youngster today. Anything is possible for a person with a keen mind. The wonders of science, art and industry are all at one's disposal. This young inventor will do England proud one day.'

'Yes, Your Highness,' said Uncle Herbert humbly.

'Yes, Your Highness,' repeated my father.

My chest swelled with pride. Prince Albert had praised me in front of my father and mother! No one would dare accuse me of wasting time on useless dreams now that I had the royal seal of approval.

The royal party moved on and the crowd broke up, eager to see more of the exhibition.

My father gazed at me, speechless for once, while my mother hugged me to her and said wonderingly, 'Perhaps the Lord *does* want you to be a scientist after all, George.'